THE MURDERER

MANIK BANDYOPADHYAY

THE MURDERER

English rendering of *Khooni* —
the last novel published posthumously

Translated from the original Bengali by

SOMDATTA MANDAL

Hawakal
PUBLISHERS
New Delhi | Calcutta

HAWAKAL PUBLISHERS PRIVATE LIMITED
70 B/9 Amritpuri, East of Kailash, New Delhi 65
33/1/2 K B Sarani, Mall Road, Calcutta 80

Email info@hawakal.com
Website www.hawakal.com

Cover Model: Sanjoy Chakraborty

Cover photograph designed by
Bitan Chakraborty

First edition September 2022

ISBN: 978-93-91431-64-8 (Paperback)

USD 13.99

for
Late Professor Dipendu Chakravarti,
my beloved teacher
who asked me to translate this novella
but could not see it in its published form

Manik Bandyopadhyay

MANIK BANDYOPADHYAY

Manik Bandyopadhyay was born on 19 May 1908 in Dumka, a small town in Santhal Parganas district in the state of Bihar in British India. His real name was Prabodh Kumar Bandyopadhyay, but owing to his dark complexion he was known to his family members as Kala Manik or Manik. He was the fifth of the fourteen children of his parents, Harihar Bandyopadhyay and Niroda Devi. Since his father was a sub-registrar posted in different parts of Bengal, Manik experienced life by living in different parts of the state. He studied at institutions in Midnapore and Bankura and in 1938 started his career as the Headmaster of Mymensingh Teachers' Training School. But throughout his life, writing was the only source of his income and hence he languished in perpetual poverty. His literary career began in 1928 with the publication of the short story "Atashi Mami" in the magazine *Bichitra* and since then his stories and novels were published in various Bengali literary magazines of the time. His famous novels like *Diba-Ratrir Kabya, Padma Nadir Majhi, Putul Nacher Itikotha* and others established him as the most notable Bengali novelist of the time, someone who distinguished himself with profound and rational analysis of the lives of ordinary people. He wrote about their pettiness and wretchedness of existence. Inspired by both Marxian as well as Freudian philosophy, his writings dealt primarily with the dark alleyways of the human mind even among the supposedly simple village folk and not the serene beauty of nature that was always in the background of his novels. In 1944, he became an active member of the Communist Party of India, studying Marx and Engles seriously. Struggling with poverty and epilepsy, Bandyopadhyay took to alcohol which added to his misery. He died an untimely death in Kolkata on 7th December 1956 at the age of forty-eight. Almost four decades after his death, the West Bengal Government published a book on his lifetime contribution to Bengali literature.

Introduction

The discovery and inclusion of this short novel in the gamut of Manik Bandyopadhyay's complete list of novels are surprising and brilliant. Written in the middle of his literary career; this novel was published in twelve instalments in a monthly journal called *Nutan Jibon* from its *Pous* 1350 B.S. to *Baisakh* 1352 B.S issues (roughly CE 1943-44). As mentioned earlier, this period also coincided with his membership in the Communist Party of India and his involvement in various socio-political events, finding its place in the writings of his time. After lying for almost half a century in oblivion, the full text of the novel was discovered and included along with other unpublished texts in the eleventh volume of his complete works published by *Paschimbanga Bangla Academy* in December 2007.

Incidentally, from his diary entries, we get to know that an attempt had been made during the author's lifetime to publish this serialized novel in book form. On 25 December 1944, the author had signed a contract with General Printers and Publishers Limited, but due to some unknown reason, it did not materialize. In the meantime, when the serial publication was collected many years later, the first three issues of the journal available in a library in North Kolkata were found to be moth-eaten and therefore, the full text could not be recovered. Though the third instalment was found in the collection of another public library, the first two still remained incomplete due to that reason. So it was in this incomplete state, with ellipsis signs (...) for the un-deciphered portions, the novel was published in 2013 by Deep Prakashan, Kolkata. This is probably the first novel in the history of publication that comes to the public domain with certain sections still incomplete. But a major portion of the missing sections can be guessed or assumed by the reader. Though unable to accommodate the corrections and revisions that the author would probably have made before publishing it in a final form — taken as a whole, the way it stands at the moment — it is not difficult for us to understand the novel per se.

This translation is a sincere attempt to bring Manik Bandyopadhyay closer to a pan-Indian and especially non-Bengali readership. It should be mentioned that although the novelist himself had changed his narrative style from the colloquial *chalitbhasha* to the more formal *sadhubhasha* somewhere in the middle of the novel by adding a footnote stating that the latter form would be a more suitable vehicle for expression, this change does not affect the translation at all. The prime goal of this translation is to maintain a uniform readability.

To conclude, along with Sunil Kumar Dhar, the editor of the monthly journal *Nutan Jibon*, the author's son Sukanta Bandyopadhyay and other family members, *Hawakal*, the publisher of this translated version, this translator also wishes all the readers of *Khooni* (*The Murderer*) to discover the genius of Manik Bandyopadhyay in a better way, despite the unprecedented limitations that this short novel upholds. Also, as mentioned earlier, attempts have been made to fill up the missing gaps in the first two sections of the text which are obvious, but in a few instances, the ellipses have been left as they are. Like most of his other novels, this short novella deals primarily with the dark alleyways of the human mind of ordinary people. Here we find the psychological ramifications within the mind of the main protagonist Mukunda, who after murdering his wife Kamini, tries to lead life according to his own terms. Also, the socialist concerns and beliefs of the author are expressed quite clearly in this novella.

Somdatta Mandal
August 2022

The Murderer

Yawning, Mukunda woke up on the bed. It was a bright morning, no nip of the winter in the air. The hesitant nature of spring seemed to have ended, and that time of the year had arrived — when summer would bid adieu to the same.

Mukunda, who was good, yet a timid soul, felt quite enlivened.

Old feelings of cheerfulness sent faint reverberations from the innumerable barriers of his mind. It was a taste of freedom of some kind. The weight seemed to have lightened, the bonding a little looser. Till now, the hangover continued, but trails of his dream were not lost in daylight. Six months ago, he fell prey to an unfortunate situation; since then, he had felt a growing pressure. He tied himself up in a strange trap that led to the lapse of his wretched fate — which should have shattered him by now. At any moment, now the palace of lies he had built might tumble down. Having kept it a secret for six months, his attempt to arrange and do the same increased each passing day — that too now needed new concealment, which could otherwise get him caught at any moment. Then why does he feel so light today?

Kamini does not know and was unaware of anything till today. But how long can Mukunda prevent her from knowing? If he does not die, then in a few days, everything will be out in the open. For her, it would be worse than death.

When he woke up at midnight, he felt that Kamini wasn't breathing — she seemed dead. He didn't know why he had that feeling. He never imagined her death. How could he even think of that! But as soon as he woke up, this was the first thing he felt. He wasn't surprised, but the thought of her death came to him very casually like any other. One wouldn't be able to differentiate whether she was asleep or had passed away.

But yes, he knew that Kamini was asleep; right from the moment till the time he felt that she was not alive, not even for a moment did he forget that she was lying next to him. Even after having realized her slumber, how could he imagine such a thing? For such a long time (...) it felt strange this morning that he did not feel anything unusual had taken place and this thought was an uncanny one!

Probably that is why it didn't feel bad. The clear knowledge of a strong and healthy woman peacefully sleeping did not make it difficult to think that she was dead, nor aroused any regrets. On some special occasions, even harmless souls are able to savour the process of such undesirable and unreasonable thoughts. The man who hesitated, when he heard of sin — not for just showing off but for a real surprise — even he could not on some occasions nurture the thought of grave sin within his mind. Because he was desperate, he tried to forget as the thought itself was sinful!

After considering the benefits of both sin and munificence and without undergoing partial heart failure, Mukunda did want to forego the wish about Kamini's death, which he could not otherwise pass as a trivial and bad thought. He did not value it much. It was like playing a joke on himself!

Had he really wanted to kill her, couldn't he have done so last night? The house had suddenly fallen empty yesterday and only both of them would be staying there for the next three days. The entire neighbourhood was silent, Kamini was in deep sleep. Couldn't he have done what he wished to do last night? For three days no one would even come to enquire what had happened to Kamini. Wasn't that enough proof that he had no ulterior motives as he had let such an opportunity go by last night? What difference would it make by just running it as a thought? People anyway dream when sleep eludes them at midnight.

Empty house! An absolutely empty one!

This morning it seemed emptier than last night. Every night after locking their door, they become all alone; the strange quietness of that night remains outside. As soon as he woke up, he heard the cacophony of the people outside. Today there wasn't any sound. Who knew what Kamini was up to!

He came downstairs and saw her scrubbing the utensils beneath the tap. Smearing toothpaste with his fingers upon his fragmented teeth Mukunda said, "I told you, I will appoint a part-time maid. Why do you have to do everything yourself?"

Kamini replied, "It's just a matter of a couple of days. Anyways it's going to cost you a lot. Drink your tea and quickly get a couple of things from the bazaar. Don't you want food before you leave for the office?"

Food for the office! For the last four years, he had been doing so religiously. But for the past six months, he was in no rush for it as he did not require any. Kamini was the one who had been dragging it on his behalf. Just because of his job, she had been paying a lot of respect to him throughout his life.

"I guess I'll skip office today."

Kamini lifted her head and looked at him.

"What has happened to you nowadays? You are not going to the office. Do you want to leave this job?"

Mukunda felt a pang in his chest. "I took leave for three days since you'll be alone. There would be no problem if Raju comes here now."

"You only forced Raju to go with them. I also thought it would be safer to stay alone at home than with a grown-up servant. Would I have let him go if I knew you had taken leave? Really, you are becoming weirder day by day."

A streak of sunlight fell on the verandah. Mukunda sipped the tea prepared by his wife, looked at it, and the thought crossed his mind whether he should tell her everything or not. Should she be told the truth and everything that has been a secret for the last six months?

His head reeled in fright. Would it be okay to let her know now? The reason for which he could not express it to Kamini at the beginning had now revved his fear a hundred-fold.

Upon hearing that there was no hurry, she slowed down with her work. Shutting the kitchen door, she went near him and said, "Since you won't be going to the office...what happened? Why did you startle?"

Staring at the broken cup, Mukunda replied, "I was thinking of something."

"Can you please take me to Manu's house today? I have to deck up a lot and go. I am yet to show her my new necklace. Last time she came and showed me her new bangles with pride — as if I didn't know that she had them made from her mother-in-law's old ornaments and not as a gift from her husband. You gave me a necklace. Why should I leave it without showing off?" Kamini smiled. "Will you take me?"

"All right," Mukunda approved.

"So then let's go. Oh, they will not let us leave without having the meal, so why should I waste time cooking? Go and shave. Give me the keys to the big trunk."

Kamini became all excited. She dragged Mukunda by his hand and made him sit in front of the big mirror to shave. She also brought him the essentials — soap, razor, etc.

Then she said, "Give me the keys. Do your shaving while I get dressed up. The poor thing will arrange for lunch only after we reach."

"Where did I keep the keys?"

As she spoke, Kamini simultaneously recalled something else. "Shall I take a bath? That's better, let us go after I take a bath. Find the keys after you finish shaving, I will be out in a moment."

Kamini would take out her jewellery from the big trunk herself. Applying the lather on his cheeks and sharpening the razor on the strap, Mukunda considered her proposal. It was surprising that it's been three months, and she didn't want to go anywhere decked up with the jewellery — so he had nothing to complain about as she wanted to do it today. In a way, this was good. Instead of opening the big trunk a couple of days ago, it was good that she would now take out her ornaments in an empty house.

After her bath, Kamini returned to find him still with lather on his cheeks as he sharpened the razor. Seeing that, she almost burst into tears.

"You still haven't finished shaving?"

Mukunda almost choked as soon as he heard her entreating tone. For someone who could become so touchy for such a simple reason, how terribly hurt she would be when she gets to know the whole thing! He has been unemployed for the past six months. Every month, Mukunda would pass on his savings and the money received by selling off her jewellery as his salary. For the past six months, he kept leaving for the office at ten in the morning. Could all these things be disclosed to Kamini?

Instead, wouldn't it be better to slit open her throat with that razor? What a soft and narrow throat she had! The sharp razor would slit it like butter.

What a brief way to find an easy solution (...) for Mukunda's consciousness (...) the split on both sides of the razor (...) After a few seconds, he thought that the entire procedure of murdering Kamini by slitting her throat was akin to cutting butter. Kamini did not move, made no sounds, did nothing, not even a drop of blood was shed from her tender throat — for the past six months the problems that Mukunda created himself and that weighed him down for every moment in his life would have no existence at all.

While looking at her throat Mukunda held out the razor and remained motionless; acknowledging his dedicated glare, Kamini felt that the man had become mesmerized by his own lather-covered beauty. She got excited. Her face became bright with the feeling of demure happiness. For a split second, the funny feeling of relief made Mukunda's body seem senseless, but at the very next moment, he was imbued with a spark.

"What are you looking at?"

Neither Kamini nor Mukunda was aware whether this mild and coy question made any difference or not. Had Kamini been a few seconds late in asking that, if necessary, the razor in Mukunda's hand would have slit her throat.

He would be shocked by the thought, 'So did I murder Kamini?' There was always some danger if he had plotted and decided wholeheartedly to do something dangerous. But there might have surfaced a moment when he stood hesitant whether to do the act or not when suddenly his eyes blacked out to the glaring sunlight. And maybe because of the coy enticement, an unknown door opened and a blind, indomitable emotion rushed out like flood. To prevent a different rush of interest, such a trivial incident like this has happened innumerable times.

"We will not go today."

Kamini was surprised and asked, "Won't I take out my saree and get ready?"

"No. Let it be!"

Kamini could not believe that Mukunda had already changed his mind. Just now, he was looking at his lather-covered face strangely, and now suddenly without saying anything, he tried to upset her by stopping their trip. Surely it was a joke.

"You just can't say let it be."

Trying to keep the situation normal, Mukunda said, "Yes, really, we can't go, Kamini. Maybe we will go some other day."

She now realized the change in his tone.

"What happened to you? When will you take me? Why not today?"

"No, I have work."

Since he was quiet, Kamini waited for a while. Then loudly she questioned again, "Why aren't you replying? You have taken leave for three days, so what work do you have now that is stopping us from visiting Manu's place?"

Mukunda could not control his temper. He yelled at her snappily, "What would you do after hearing it? I am saying I have work, that's it."

At first, Kamini became puzzled a bit by his sudden and illogical anger. On listening to her innocent, good-natured husband, who had never spoken in a harsh tone, and now as he suddenly splintered out like gunpowder, she thought it to be a dream. But Kamini didn't spend much time in surprise. He had prevented her wishes. On top of that, instead of offering explanations, he was screaming.

She said, "Who do you think you're talking to, huh?"

(...)

"Tell me, who do you think I am?"

Suddenly Mukunda's anger surged; the guy, who was known to be a timid person, was no longer the same one. An intolerable pain stemming from hatred started welling inside him like fireworks. He seemed to have lost all tolerance when a little bit of blood oozed out while he was shaving, and now he was desperately fuming with anger. This Kamini was his enemy, the curse upon his life. What an unbelievable affair it was that he had kept the news of losing his job from her because she would be in distress. He was almost losing it to have kept the news, a secret one, from her month after month.

Maybe if she could see Mukunda's face, the bickering would have stopped. But he sat with his back towards her while one of his cheeks remained covered with the soap lather. After a few altercations, he forcefully fell silent, but Kamini went on shouting severely at her husband.

Before his anger surged to its fullest, taking out his beautiful walking stick he suddenly began beating his wife. The first three strikes hit Kamini's shapely youthful body, the same one which all this while would arouse Mukunda even if he imagined touching it. Kamini kept on wailing and fell. After hitting her head for the fourth time, she lost consciousness. With all his might, he clasped Kamini's throat with both hands, and like a lunatic started shaking her.

Before she could even sense his deception, Mukunda hit her hard on the head. He did not even remember why he murdered her or the exact reason for doing so. He couldn't understand what happened to him, so he thought of slitting her butter-like throat into two — found it to be the easiest method to silence her.

(…)

Doctor Abhoy gave the certificate. He was in the medical profession for ten or twelve years but failed to achieve great heights. He was not Mukunda's friend, but they'd known each other for a long time.

Mukunda did not call Abhoy. After lifting and laying her down on the bed, Mukunda sat quietly, thinking about what to do next. He had that much sense that he had to do something, but didn't know what. Almost like reciting a poem by heart, he kept thinking about what should be done now. After he had spent three hours in such a state, Doctor Abhoy came to his house.

The latter gave him a loan. About four days prior to this, he asked for it, and Mukunda said that he would repay it today. This was the only connection between the arrival of the Doctor and Kamini's murder three hours earlier.

Upon seeing the doctor at the front door, Mukunda knew what he had to do. Though the thought came to his mind suddenly, he did not resort to abruptness. It seemed as if everything was planned.

"She is very sick, Abhoy babu. It's good that you have come."

"What sickness?"

"She fainted suddenly, and after that, she seemed to have become unconscious. She is hardly breathing."

Abhoy was startled. "What are you saying? Come, let's go and have a look."

"Come."

Mukunda's exhausted face made Abhoy a bit suspicious. He had never seen such a complacent demeanour and such lack of anxiety in someone whose wife had fallen unconscious.

Walking next to the bed, Abhoy stood quietly for a minute. Observing Kamini's neck and head, he looked at Mukunda and realized that the latter was waiting for the doctor's reply.

The doctor took out his stethoscope and after examining her said, "Mukunda babu, she is not alive."

"Not alive? What do you mean?"

"After growing senseless, she died — of heart failure."

'Really? Abhoy babu, are you telling the truth?" Mukunda's dim eyes brightened up. "So, I have not murdered her?"

"Let that be."

Mukunda was depressed again after hearing from the doctor. He trusted Abhoy. Believing that Kamini had died on her own, that he had not killed her, even after getting excited and mentioning the murder, he wasn't nervous. Now, after realizing that the doctor wasn't playing with him, tears ran down his cheeks. Being flabbergasted, he tried to control it.

"Mukunda babu, please control yourself."

He shut his eyes.

Only firm will can overcome brewing discomfort in one's mind. Mukunda gnashed and was unable to speak.

"Arrange for about five hundred rupees."

"Five hundred rupees? Where will I get it?"

"OK." Abhoy put the stethoscope in his pocket. "Open her bangles and the necklace. Take out whatever is there in the box."

Mukunda kept on looking in wonder.

Without losing his complacency, the doctor said, "Would your staring be enough to suffice? Shouldn't she be taken to the crematorium? I am arranging everything."

The local workers of Sukarma Sangha took Kamini to the crematorium. Being a married woman, her neck, face, and head were almost covered with sindoor and coloured powder. This was done as Abhoy advised.

Mukunda also went with them. When the pyre started burning steadily, he moved away. After roaming here and there, he landed at the temple in Kalighat. Sitting in the courtyard with his legs folded on a wooden bench, he saw a goat being sacrificed and remembered that he had to buy a goat for the workers of Sukarma Sangha — one goat, and two bottles. He didn't have any cash. He needed to inform Abhoy. Putting his feet down from the bench, he noticed that his shoes were gone. Then he remembered that when he left home for the crematorium, he was barefoot.

Mukunda felt a great relief. The shoes were not lost. He had only one pair of them, and had they been lost or stolen, he would then be in trouble.

The question of what to do next had not yet been resolved. As he stood up, Mukunda realized that he did not know where to go and what to do. It seemed as if all his responsibilities in life were over, there was no reason for staying alive. For the first time in his life, he became conscious of a strange, unbearable feeling. It was the end of his life, a weightless vacuum. He had undergone both physical and mental pain, but those were not similar to the unexplained feelings that cropped up today. It did not seem like a pain — this feeling had no rhythm, no rise or fall, no sharpness. It was an unexplained condition when he felt light as air and at the same time felt pressure both on the inside and the outside.

As he started walking, Mukunda shook his head seriously. Let there be sorrow and suffering. O God, let him suffer, let heart-rendering sorrow arise. He could not tolerate the silence. As he walked past the clay dolls sold in a shop, he looked at all the beggars lined up in a row and felt that amidst the crowd of living human beings, he too was one of those clay figures. He wasn't himself as he walked. The feet were not his. The body was not his. He did not exist.

Was he alive? Did he not die? These thoughts seemed quite laughable but at the same time, did not seem impossible. He did not feel a bit eager to verify whether he was dead or alive. No matter, the more conscious he tried to be about his well-known associations, the less realistic everything appeared, more dubious like a dream.

He had stopped in front of a shop that sold flowers and garlands, and after bumping into a guy, he stopped and resumed walking. Crossing the tram line junction, he took the road next to the canal and went on without knowing where or why he was going. He swayed and walked a little. Dinesh came from behind and after seeing his condition, spoke sarcastically, "You have drunk so much already?"

When Mukunda had a job, among his fellow workers, this Dinesh was his closest associate.

As Mukunda turned, even in the faint light of the evening, Dinesh's smile disappeared as he looked at him.

"What happened, Mukunda?"

"Brother, my wife passed away."

"Died? When?"

"This morning. She suddenly fainted and then died of heart failure. Cremated her just now."

"Gosh! All of a sudden!" Saying that Dinesh stood like a dumb person while expressing his heartfelt sympathy.

"Were you going for a drink? In that same shop?" Mukunda asked.

"Yes. What about you?"

"I was also going for a drink."

It was a lie. There was indeed a country liquor shop nearby, and a long time back, Mukunda had once been there with Dinesh. But he did not even think about having a drink before he met Dinesh. Anyhow, they went to that liquor shop and drank for a while; eventually, Mukunda tumbled from the wooden bench on which they were sitting. Dinesh lifted him, put him up on a rickshaw, and took him to a woman in a nearby shanty. Looking at the condition of Mukunda, the woman said, "Why don't you die?"

Mukunda used to work in Dhandas Dutta's office.

Compared to his business, the office was a relatively small one and worked with limited people. Dhandas refused to hire extra hands.

Work went on. Incessantly.

Dhandas had a few simple methods through which he monitored that no one could be a little lax in their work. First of all, every work in his office was important — urgent — to be done immediately. Sometimes it would take seven days to complete a task, while at other times, a task would be taken off the hook within seven days. He wanted to complete it within two days. Of course, he knew that it was impossible, and he did not have the zest of turning the impossible into reality. He was happy if the work took five days to complete instead of seven, though he showed great dissatisfaction so that the employee would be ashamed and grow fearful thinking about his incapability and would be motivated to work harder. But even after everything, if the work was found incomplete within seven days, then on top of that the employee would be burdened with additional work. No matter how much he tried, he could never complete his work; there were always extra ones. So, there was also no dearth of trying.

Secondly, everyone had to enter the office by

ten and sign their names in the register. One had to explain for late arrival -- after ten-thirty, it would be considered late, and after eleven, absent. Absent, but so what? Even after one arrived and was marked absent, what was the harm in working? After all, the work must be completed.

The tiffin break was for half an hour — from one to one-thirty. It was exactly by the clock — not too less, nor too much. Almost every day a little later after one o'clock noon, Dhandas would stroll around the office. With a smile, he spoke one or two words to those who remained in their seats and were found having tea and snacks. So, most of the office staff had stopped taking their tiffin break. Those who went outside did not stay there for more than five or seven minutes.

The office would be over at five pm. Everyone was free to leave then, and no one to prevent. But if Dhandas himself, or his I.C.S. failed manager Dinesh, or his secretary Manilal was still there in the office, did it look nice for the lower-class employees to leave before them? Wasn't that some sort of an insult to the superiors? It was an unsaid imperative to inform them. If you went to let them know, then Dhandas or Dinesh or Manilal would say, "Is it past five o'clock? OK, you can leave."

Just as the employee was about to leave, Dhandas or Dinesh or Manilal would add, "Listen. Please take this file. I want this tomorrow before noon. And if you need some other files, they are all there with Jadav babu. Don't lose them."

So, who could dare to prepare the statement

without working till midnight and then again from six to nine in the morning?

Thus, the office ran on a system, men did not run it.

The arrangement of Dhandas's friend Raichand was different. He kept more employees but offered them less pay.

He would say, "You are wrong. If you make them work more, will the output be larger? Isn't there a capacity for working? If they get tired, then they'd take two hours to complete the job instead of one, there would be more mistakes."

Dhandas replied, "You know nothing. I have heard this quite a lot. Those people themselves go on passing around that idea. They come to work with plenty of education and go on publishing articles in newspapers about how less labour increases the volume of work."

Dhandas had an insurance company along with a bank and transport business. All of them functioned well.

One day Dhandas got hold of a press quite cheap, which someone had sold off due to loans and liabilities. He would have earned quite a large profit if he sold it, but Dhandas thought that the press was not like fish and that it would become stale overnight and incur losses. When several people were making a profit by running presses, he could also try and run this press properly and see how the business was and what the profit and loss would be like. If he did not like it, he could always sell it off.

Dhandas was thinking about all this and after

consulting a friend, who owned a press as well, he would arrange a procedure for running his press. One day, while leaving in his car for the office at around ten am, he suddenly saw Mukunda walking along the footpath.

He stopped the car on one side of the road and sent his driver to fetch Mukunda.

"How are you Mukunda babu? Is everything all right?"

"Yes, I am fine."

Having unkempt hair, an unshaved beard, and a moustache on his face, Mukunda wore a dirty shirt and a clean dhoti and wore a pair of ladies sandals, which belonged to Kamini. He was looking slightly like a lunatic.

"You look like a poet. Are you writing a lot? Oh no, I heard that you lost your wife."

"Yes, sir."

After an awkward silence, he responded quite shyly, "No, I have never written any poems. I had the habit of writing a little prose..."

"Oh, it's the same thing. Prose and poetry, how does it matter? Are you working anywhere?"

"No, sir."

"Didn't you have a press, before you came to work at my office?"

"I didn't open it exactly. It was a partnership with a friend. All the money I had went into that."

Dhandas pondered over and said, "Why don't you come to my office once? I have bought a press and was wondering whether to employ you."

Mukunda was quite excited to hear that and asked, "Do you have time today?"

"Yes, come around at three o'clock."

Even after Dhandas's car moved along with other cars and finally disappeared, Mukunda kept standing there. His ears felt hot with this sudden excitement. Once Dhandas had sacked him out of the blue. Mukunda didn't have a job for six months. That is why he had to murder Kamini. And now Dhandas was offering him a job again. To his surprise, he chanced upon it while walking down the street.

Did he murder Kamini? He had only hit her with the stick while he was furious. He didn't wish for that.

After he started working in Dhandas's press, Mukunda felt a strange transformation within him. It seemed as if from the desperate condition he was gradually becoming more lethargic, and the long process of tiding over the terrible haze of a distressing dream had begun. The exasperation intensified because of the accumulated stress, which was slowly brewing within him; a violent frenzy was slowly fading away. For all these days, Mukunda did not realize that he had been going through such a strange situation. From the time of Kamini's death till now, he had considered himself a very timid, worn out, half-dead immobile creature. He would be happy to rest his head somewhere and fall asleep. Due to a lack of the spirit to live his life, his body temperature reduced to a level where he shivered like a patient with a fever.

But now, after undergoing so much tedious labour in the press when he was exhausted, he realized that all this while he was like a bomb packed with excitement and not like a deflated balloon with a vacuum.

For how long has he been in this condition? Mukunda felt as if he was like this from birth. He understood that it was not the truth, and it was impossible. But this unending aberration had engulfed his past in such a manner that he could not in any way remember since when he had lost his mind. Was it from the time of Kamini's death? Was it from the time he lost his job, secretly selling her ornaments and getting an amount that he passed as his salary to Kamini at the beginning of every month? Or was it even earlier when Dhandas had suddenly sacked him from his job?

Who knew!

Nowadays, occasionally he had also started grieving for Kamini. This affair made him uncomfortable. Without any reason, his weary body would suddenly become paralysed, and the light in front of his eyes would turn dim. Uncontrollable despair for Kamini would hover within his body like a suppressed whine. He felt like wailing blaringly and even wanted to roll on the ground. So, Kamini appeared in his mind under a different garb. Sometimes he would be so engrossed in his thoughts about her that he would unknowingly forget his distress. After regaining his consciousness, he found himself to have overcome that situation and had no trace of gloom left in his mind. Even if he tried to be sad by remembering Kamini, he no longer felt despair as his senses had turned blunt.

Again, suffering would emerge all of a sudden in

a similar process. The thoughts of Kamini would also eventually disappear.

This was how his days were being spent. Mukunda spoke less and worked more. And at different places and times, he would stare at the faces of both known and unknown people with the inquisitiveness of a small child. He tried to understand what that person was thinking and why he was thinking.

Even Dhandas felt uncomfortable in the presence of Mukunda's strange countenance.

The work of the press was going on quite well, and he had nothing to say about it. But Dhandas was perpetually dissatisfied over everything. So he tried to say, "Mukunda babu, I find that everybody leaves exactly by the clock."

"Yes, sir. The rules of the factory are very strict. You got to pay extra if you want to detain them for a long time."

"Oh, I have seen such rules a lot."

"Sir, in the office, the rules are different. This is a factory, and so we cannot ask anyone to stay back after the said time."

"It can be said if you know how to say it."

Mukunda kept quiet. Dhandas came to the press at late hours, just before the time was over for the day. Soon the rattling sound of the machines would stop. The workers in the press would finish their work and begin washing their hands with soap. Dhandas would be irritated and say, "It seems they are in a hurry to leave."

Mukunda did not reply.

Very little light entered through the window in

this office room of the press, so the lights had to be switched on. Looking at the dissatisfied mark on Dhandas's shrewd and cruel face, Mukunda suddenly felt that the man's life was very brittle. The signs of death seemed to have been engraved in his watery eyes, swollen cheeks, and discoloured skin. It was much easier to kill him than Kamini.

Of course, it was true that Mukunda had no reason to kill Dhandas.

This was a meaningless and irrelevant thought. There was no reason to toy with the idea in his mind. Like bubbles emanating from the depths of a deep lake, a lot of unusual thoughts surfaced in a man's mind and then disappeared once again. Who kept track of it? What did it bother others? Dhandas had helped him. He had given him a job once again. Mukunda regretted that he could not discover that gratitude within himself. But at the same time, he could not get rid of the idea of killing Dhandas from his mind.

No, he didn't want to. He just thought about how easy it would be to kill him. As soon as Dhandas appeared before his eyes, he could see the signs of death on his face — as if imminent death came in the guise of sleep that was stuck upon his face. Looking at Kamini's soft, well-shaped and smooth butter-like neck, he thought that his sharp razor could slice it easily like cutting through air or water. But nowadays, Dhandas's dry, shriveled, and lean neck could be broken by just holding it tight with his bare hands.

Dhandas felt very uncomfortable with the way

Mukunda looked at him.

"What are you gaping at?"

"Nothing sir." Mukunda was startled, and he blinked several times and shook his head.

"Did you hear what I said?"

"Yes, sir. I have heard."

Dhandas was unwilling to believe. But he found that Mukunda had heard and understood everything. The former then tried to smile a little, and said, "From your behaviour it seems as if your mind is someplace else. Do you live alone?"

"Servants are there."

After keeping quiet for a while, Dhandas said, "It is enough Mukunda babu. Now get married once again. Even after enduring grief, man must go on living. How can you yield to fate? If you had children, it was something else. Since you've none, you should therefore marry a nice young girl."

"Marry? What are you saying?"

Dhandas grew a bit ashamed and annoyed at seeing Mukunda's extreme eagerness. What sort of love for his wife was this? Four or five months had already gone by, and now everything would be all right if he settled into domesticity once again like a timid and good man. Dhandas also knew of a woman. She was dark-skinned and limped on one leg, but she was quite a grown-up and would be able to shoulder all domestic responsibilities immediately after marriage. Dhandas would also feel lighter if he got married to her.

After he left, Mukunda sat down and kept running the thought of his boss's desire. Nowadays, even the slightest elation dawned like absurdity to him. The first question that popped in his mind was about Dhandas's intention. Why was he so keen to get Mukunda married to someone else just after Kamini's death? Dhandas himself did not plan to kill her so that he could get another girl to marry him. Then why did he employ Mukunda and plead the latter to marry again just three months after his wife's death?

Mukunda felt that he was harboring such thoughts in an unsound mind. It didn't seem logical. After reinstating him in his job, Dhandas might have thought that since this man's wife was dead, he could thrust another girl on him as his wife. But it was ridiculous to imagine that the boss had planned his marriage beforehand and then appointed him to his job. Despite realizing this, Mukunda went on weaving all these meaningless thoughts. He even had this haughty hope in his mind that if things went on like this, at one point in time, he would be able to unravel another murderer of Kamini.

He had discovered this right at the beginning, but it could not be brought out in the open. He was digging into logic to make the discovery convincing enough. Otherwise, why would Dhandas offer him the job in the very first place? Was it just because he wanted to somehow thrust this girl upon her? But the idea of thrusting this girl upon Mukunda's shoulders after getting Kamini murdered, and thereafter offering the job, didn't seem to fit right.

It seemed as if Dhandas could not sleep peacefully at night because of him.

But it was also true that if the boss did not fire

him, Mukunda would not have killed Kamini.

It was just a matter of coincidence.

He even knew that it wasn't logical for one to murder his wife just because he had lost his job. Then thousands of killings of such kinds would take place. A lot of people lose their jobs, but would it mean that they would go around killing their wives? It was just a wrong act, acted out of nothing but hard luck.

Dhandas was not to be blamed. Since this resulted after Dhandas sacked Mukunda from his job, and the latter could not help by not killing Kamini — this was the bare truth. But Dhandas could no longer be involved in this respect.

Did Mukunda murder Kamini? No, he did not murder her. He had no intention of doing so. Kamini had an illness, and she died suddenly.

Mukunda gradually became more and more emaciated. He had lost his appetite, and even after he ate, he faced trouble digesting. He did not realize that the fat in his body had reduced a lot, but he understood his physical weakness sometimes when his head reeled. His lack of sleep was the biggest problem.

He could not understand clearly whether he spent his nights sleeping or staying awake. Doing so, a series of pictures hovered in his mind, even in his dream, there would be pictures — it became difficult to differentiate between thoughts and dreams. Of course, it was indefinable that he did make serious attempts to distinguish between the two. He didn't require it.

One day Dhandas asked him, "What is the

matter? Why has your face turned out like this?"

On hearing it, Mukunda lost his cool. "Why, what has happened to my face?"

"What has happened? You have dried up like a skeleton. Consult a doctor immediately. Have you got tuberculosis?"

Mukunda's fingers were restlessly trembling. Like a spellbound person, he silently kept on staring at Dhandas's dry and shriveled neck.

After the latter left, distressing fear like the thick fog on a winter evening started accumulating in Mukunda's mind. Is it true what Dhandas said? Has he been inflicted by tuberculosis? Impossible!

He could feel that he had grown skinny, but could not comprehend to what level. But skeleton-like? However emaciated he might be, could he look like a skeleton — was he so handsome? It was impossible.

As he sat on the chair, he kept pressing the armrest with both his hands. The strange glare of his deep black eyes seemed to blink in rhythm. The repeated sounds of the different printing machines appeared like listening to strange heartbeats through a stethoscope that was not similar to the uniform heartbeats of men. A faint light came in from the small black window that could just turn the darkness inside into a hazy shadow, the light from the bare yellow bulbs resembled the dim vision of a jaundiced patient. There was a damp earthy smell resembling a sensation when one drinks water from a rotten ditch.

The sweeper Ganesh came and said, "Babu, you need to turn off the machines."

"Why?"

"They have heated up."

"Let it be."

"The machines would start malfunctioning, babu."

Ganesh had a wide forehead, his cheeks were a bit swollen, his nose and chin quite blunt, and his eyes were brownish like a cat. He would shave only twice or thrice a month, and then the black pock marks from pimples would become more prominent on his face.

"Nothing will happen, we'll keep running it."

Ganesh fumbled and said, "The boss will kill us, babu. The machine will be damaged if you run it relentlessly. And the boss is not going to like that."

"Keep on running the machine. Let it be on."

He went and visited the compositors' room. Lochan, Mona, Harish, and Kunu frequently suffered from bouts of fever, and finding all four of them present today surprised Mukunda. He looked at the dry skin on their faces, their dull placid eyes, their dry hands full of veins, and their way of sitting in a hunchback manner and then tried to discover their similarity with a skeleton-like emaciated appearance. He also tried to figure out whether they showed any signs of tuberculosis. Was he thinner than all of them? Was he frailer than them?

"Lochan, are you working with fever? Your eyes look bloodshot."

"What can I do, babu?"

Mukunda felt perturbed. He was unable to understand something, grasp what was the matter. He remembered his name at one moment, but at the very next moment could not remember it anymore. The shrewdest experience of his life seemed to resurface faintly and practically in others but more so clearer through these four patients. But like a man with his eyes shut, he could feel the presence of light but could not see anything. Lochan said, "What can I do, babu?" He came down to work with a fever. He had his wife and probably also children at home. Therefore, he had no option other than working; otherwise, his wife and children would starve to death. But what was the similarity between the sick Lochan reporting to work even with fever so that his wife and children wouldn't starve to death and Mukunda murdering his wife because he had no job?

"Lochan, how many children do you have?"

"Sir, I am unmarried."

The matter appeared irrelevant. As he sat on his chair, he thought again, trying to overcome new terrors and fresh uneasiness. When the gatekeeper brought the post, Mukunda suddenly became very annoyed after looking at his plump and healthy countenance. He desperately started looking for an excuse to curse him on any pretext whatsoever. On other occasions, he found so many reasons to get annoyed, but now he could not remember anything. Even the gatekeeper started to leave quietly after he looked at Mukunda.

Mukunda then exploded like a bomb.

"Where are you going, you monkey? Why are you leaving without informing, you bastard?"

The poor gatekeeper also retaliated to this

unnecessarily indecent attack, and to this Mukunda, instantly dismissed him.

On his way home, he eagerly tried to find out the uncontrollable truth in the faces of all sickly and skinny persons what he had somewhat realized in the compositor's room of the press. His forever self-centred mind suddenly became conscious of the existence of innumerable other human beings. No philosophical data arose in his mind, he only thought that he had a way of gaining some knowledge about himself among several other sick and depressed people, and he should know it. After returning home, he started looking very consciously at the small mirror, which he used for shaving to discover how lean he had become. If he looked attentively, then as had always happened, his face appeared unfamiliar to him — the face he had known forever and saw every day gave rise to an inevitable unknown mystery that could not be resolved.

Then Mukunda suddenly remembered that big mirror, which he'd bought for Kamini to dress up. He could see not only his face but also his full body in that mirror.

For all these days, he did not unlock this room even once, which had all the belongings of Kamini. Maybe she was there, and for a split second, he had also enjoyed the taste of this bitter falsehood he had lived with that struck like a lightning.

Mukunda opened the door and went inside. He turned on the light. Instead of being conscious of the innumerable memorabilia of Kamini, he went and stood straight in front of the mirror and began undressing. He hadn't taken off his clothes after returning from the office.

The mirror was covered with a layer of dust. To see himself clearly, he didn't look at his image but first cleaned the mirror with the dhoti he was wearing.

Seeing his well-known naked body, single and lonely after quite a long time, he turned his head and called, "Hey! Are you listening? Come quickly, dear!"

After murdering her six months back, Mukunda entered their damp, and empty bedroom full of cobwebs, and to get rid of the unaccustomed loneliness, he eagerly reached out for Kamini. He held out his hand as if searching and trying to hold the tender hand of his non-existent wife.

They would hold hands and come together to stand in front of the mirror. Both he and Kamini would create a wonderful and pretty picture of complete union in reality in the presence of that piece of glass. Apart from seeing each other, standing together side by side emanated a sense of inexpressible peace and contentment, the ultimate realization of the great union of life. After that, they embraced and rubbed their cheeks against each other. Then they would silently stare at the mirror, feeling a profound sense of indivisibility. Strange enough, every time Mukunda would feel that both of them gave life to the grammatical simile of saturation he had learned in his college days.

Kamini could not tolerate it for long. She would gradually close her eyes, bend her head, and sink it onto Mukunda's shoulders. With that weight, he realized how her body became exhausted. In bed, she would lie in a comatose fashion and would not respond even when she was called. She loved Mukunda so much that she would surrender her body, mind, and consciousness to him. Her slim and glorious body in bed radiated self-effacement in such a way that it aroused an undefined sorrow in Mukunda's heart. After his intoxicated state of self-gratification was worn out, he took himself to be a coarse human being with only physical sensibilities and deemed himself unfit for the unearthly wealth of Kamini. One after the other, he could recall his wife's innumerable habits, relating to natural cleanliness and gracefulness.

He recollected her image of pleasant purity after she took her early morning bath, worshiped her gods with flowers and sandalwood paste, the incense-scented welcome in the evening, her controlled and limited intake of food, her light rhythm of movement, faint and pleasant smile, the jingling tone of her words and her shedding of sympathetic tears. He was not the appropriate person for appreciating her beauty, her mind, or her heart. Mukunda's heart grieved intensely. He had loved Kamini like a man of flesh and blood, and as if for repentance he would slowly caress her unconscious body lying in bed by smelling the perfume in her hair, carefully kiss her whole body, and worship her by staring at her face with an overwhelmed and lamentable glare. The deep silence of midnight would sometimes be interrupted for him with different kinds of rhythmic sounds. Even his eyes felt difficulty adjusting to the static brightness of the electric bulb in the room that sparked now and then.

So, this was his playroom. Everything else was exactly as it was earlier, only his playmate was missing. The folded sarees, petticoats, and blouses hung from the clothes stand, and three pairs of sandals were kept side by side. On the dressing table, rested her hair ribbons, hairpins, powders, creams, a box of sindoor, and a bottle of oil. The bedcover was dark green, while one pillow made him reminisce how Kamini put her head on it. The white embroidered cover decorating the wedding trunk and the khaki-colored cover of the suitcase were both made by her. She even fixed the hole in the mosquito net, which resulted from Mukunda's cigarette. She wanted to hang a calendar on the wall and had hurt her finger while trying to fix a nail with the grinding pestle. She felt ashamed to let someone see her cry, so she made a strange face.

Mukunda looked at everything in a baffled manner. She found Kamini in all the small and big, useful and useless things that lay everywhere. He also found her in his personal belongings. Looking at his folded dhoti, he recalled how swift her fingers worked as it wafted before his eyes; he recollected how Kamini would stand next to the bed folding all the dry clothes while making a rhythmic sound when she intermittently hit the bed with her left knee. She would slip her left palm into one of his shoes, sit on her haunches, and brush it. As she bent, her blouse would tighten up, and as a result, her bosoms would be visible.

The happiness that she felt while brushing his shoes led to reverberation of rhythm in her body. Kamini's memories emanated in mind that dazzled to and fro, from left and right, from up and low, and at an angle as well as on a smooth surface. The entire house with all its furniture and her memory linked to them was disappearing rhythmically in a distant land of darkness. There amidst the burning pyre Kamini burnt in a saree, and here he witnessed the perfect and lovely body of his nude wife lying in front of him. He felt like pulling her close.

"Syphilis?" Mukunda did not bat an eyelid in anger or surprise. "You doctors are worthless. Why on earth would I be diagnosed with syphilis? All my life, I have never even looked at a prostitute."

His doctor friend replied quite casually, "Maybe. But you can get syphilis, even if you don't sleep with a sex worker."

Mukunda was a little hurt and looked at his friend. "You think I have been seeing some other woman? I am now twenty-eight years old, and I promise you brother that I never had any bad relationship with any woman."

"It might be so. But without that also, you can have syphilis. Though generally, people believe that it happens one way, it is not the case. One might get it transmitted from someone else. That does not mean, one must come close or get into contact with that person. You can be drinking tea in a restaurant, and someone might leave syphilis for you in that cup. But the disease spreads little in this manner. In most cases, a man or a woman transmits it to one another, and the children inherit that from their parents. I don't know about you, but you will need long-term treatment by a specialist doctor. And let me tell you something else — don't hide anything.

Mukunda didn't seem to hear those words and gave a bewildered reply, "Syphilis? I have got syphilis? I didn't get to know about it, and I have got syphilis?"

"How will you be aware of it? You were confident that one cannot be diagnosed with syphilis unless he visited a prostitute. Maybe you had rashes all over your body and thought it was simply a skin disease. But you should know, it is a very erratic and roughish disease. It manifests itself in some people very clearly, but for others, it stays suppressed in such a manner that it becomes difficult for an ordinary person to concede it. Again, in some cases, it reveals itself over the years in the guise of different kinds of diseases. Due to little or no attention, a lot of people are left untreated in the early stages. As a result, the disease becomes a serious one, and the treatment likewise becomes full of hassles. Is it only that? In the meantime, without knowing anything, he digs the grave in society — transmits the disease to his wife leading to the birth of a deformed, crippled, and blind child. Mukunda, you have no idea what a great curse it is to society." After remaining quiet for some time, the doctor added, "But why are you so upset? It is good for you that at least it has been detected. You will be cured after treatment."

"Shall I be cured? Some people say that syphilis is never completely cured."

"That is the problem. People make such statements without knowing anything. This is the greatest symptom — ignorance. Someone who doesn't know anything has a great advantage in this respect — he is dispassionate. He goes on to say whatever comes to his mind without bothering about whether it is right or wrong. You can see this everywhere. Someone who doesn't know anything speaks a thousand times louder and with more conviction than someone who knows about it. But you are an educated, intelligent person —"

Mukunda stopped him and said, "Don't talk about education brother. Let that go to hell. I am thinking of something else. How did you suspect me?"

The doctor replied, "I have already told you about the different disguises this disease can take. That day you suddenly fainted. It could be due to physical weakness, mental strain, etc. but in your case, rest can be assured only after undergoing a medical test."

After Mukunda's face turned pale, he hung his head. It was difficult for him to even imagine the matter. In his mind, he had forever felt a terrible abhorrence regarding this disease and believed that man diagnosed it as penance for a material sin. But it was a terrible feeling on his part to have gotten it. Apart from this, another fearful thought crossed his mind that belittled the attack of the illness on his body.

On that day, he had fainted not because of the unbearable mental suffering for Kamini but because of syphilis! No doubt he had suffered for her, but the disease was the reason behind his fainting. If that was true, his entire past turned deceitful for him. All his happiness and sorrow, his life full of success and failure was just an aberration of life and for all this while this unknown and invisible enemy had been playing with him like a puppet on the stage of life. Just as alcohol enlivens the drunkard, tainted syphilis has kept him active in joy and despair. Even the thought of it made Mukunda's head reel. So, were all the happy years spent together a lie? If his despair for her was an aberration, his love for her was also similar.

Gradually Mukunda started realizing that along with Kamini, the purpose for his living had also ended; he was bereft of purpose to stay alive. Today he understood that it was a mistake. There was at least some meaning to somehow survive in life by seething in pain for Kamini, whom he had killed with his own hands. Today he got to know that his life was meaningless. But his life had not ended — this was because he did not have anything called a personal life.

Though he knew that asking questions was useless, he gathered courage within his mind and asked the doctor, "So, was that a syphilitic stroke I had that day when I fainted?"

The doctor thought for a while and replied, "No. But syphilis was also responsible. I know everything, so it was easy for me to say it. It would be difficult for other doctors. I told you earlier that you could have fainted because of the strain you had endured for six or seven months, along with the weak body that you have. But don't take the responsibility for the disease lightly. Maybe—"

"Maybe?"

"Why maybe, let me tell you that it is the truth. The reactions that you have had for your wife would not have been so strong if you didn't have the disease."

Mukunda did not get much consolation after listening to the doctor's explanation. But he got some amount of mental satisfaction from the thought that however weak he might be, he had not succumbed to the disease.

It was biting cold. Except for the smog in the morning and evening, the daytime in the city was a bright one. The birds flying in the clear sky appeared like floating black dots. With a soft quilt at night and some warm clothes during the day, the body felt comfortable. A lot of new fruits and vegetables had arrived in the market and the fortunate people were savouring the delicacies with delight. However little that might be, many weak ones had turned healthy by having better quality food. Only some people with rough, chapped skin and cracked lips without a smile, endured the sharp pangs of winter, their shriveled nerves quivered with the lack of warmth. By the time they finished basking in the sunshine to get rid of the cold, the dreadful night dawned upon them. Before falling off to sleep, the fire they had lit up by collecting twigs, dry leaves, and garbage would smother itself. So it was back to wrapping their bodies with torn rags and quilts and rived jute mats, curling themselves like dogs, eagerly waiting for the morning to arrive.

Mukunda did not know that in this humid

country, such an awful lot suffered during winter.

Narayan Acharya, his next-door neighbour, said with a mild smile, "There is so much rain in Bengal. But did you know that many people here suffer from lack of water?" The seriousness in his eyes did not lighten his smile. Earlier Mukunda would feel offended if anyone hinted that he did not know about something, and he would desperately feel the urge and try to prove that he was knowledgeable about everything. Now he felt ashamed that he hardly knew anything about things that were to be known in the world.

Narayan said that everyone should know at least something about the condition of our country.

"Surely, was there any doubt about it?"

Mukunda replied sincerely but not with exuberance. There was a healthy glow on his face. The depression and self-accusation vanished from his face, and he was devoid of limitless excitement in his behaviour. The permanent distortion of his face induced by pain could even make a stranger imagine that he was suffering from colic pain or toothache and that same face was now totally calm, revealing a quiet and satisfied look. Mukunda no longer stayed alone, he did not think of things at random, did not create great turmoil in his mind, and enjoyed all of it.

It was not that his untamed mind was now totally under his control, or he was able to do away with his mental anxieties altogether. The prolonged treatment of the difficult ailment through a controlled lifestyle, his dedication to purify his own poisonous body, the idea of bringing in a revolution in his entire life — the great hurt and gradual reaction of his practical experience and many more things had brought a change of course in his life. He was shocked in the beginning and felt the deep despair that instead of living, it was better to commit suicide. While he nurtured this thought of committing suicide, he suddenly realized something that shocked him with horror.

In the depraved mind of his sick body, Mukunda had thought that he had killed his wife. Doesn't the idea of killing oneself arise from the same diseased mind once again? His mind was not in the normal condition, and if not completely, at least he was partly like a lunatic. Did he have the capacity to decide what was right and what was wrong? The desire to end his unsuccessful life and his toxic body might be a resultant symptom of his disease.

Fear had turned Mukunda clueless. If his mind was rotten, all his small and big thoughts and feelings were also distorted. Ideas were false, his happiness and despair contrived, and every moment of his life was a simple betrayal. The terrible pain he underwent before he fainted in front of the mirror seemed to have turned him insane once again with contorted self-realization.

He was unable to sense how much he screamed at the top of his voice and converted his blind desire to just run away in an irate way towards his doctor friend.

—"What happened, Mukunda?"

—"Have I turned insane? Don't lie to me. I

earnestly request you not to hoodwink me. Tell me the truth. Have I been insane for a long time?"

"No."

"How do you know?"

"Sit down and listen. Once you hear me out, you will understand. A man who goes nuts never thinks about whether he is insane or not. For some suspicion brewing in his mind can make him question the same — turning a maniac is impossible."

Mukunda sat quietly for a long time.

"Even if I am not insane, is my mind in a state of aberration?" Mukunda asked him and kept on staring at his friend's face.

"The answer to your question cannot be a brief one. I don't know how many unperturbed minds there are in this world, but I haven't come across anyone much like that. Of course, some people have more aberrations, some less."

"Surely, do I have a lot of it within me?"

His friend hesitated for a while and replied, "It can be possible."

From that point onward, the vehemence of his frenzy lessened a bit. His doctor friend had told him several times that he would be cured if he underwent prolonged treatment. Mukunda thought if that was the case, he should patiently wait to see what would come out in the end. Probably his mind would also get cured along with his body.

At the point when his knowledge was enamored by

deception and couldn't choose unadulterated and impure sentiments inside his mind, he wouldn't partake in any unnecessary thoughts. He would make a point of bliss, distress, desire, wishes, exhaustion, lament, dread, downfall, and despairing to be taken care of. He would even try and forget everything till his body and mind was fully recovered. Who knew whether his distress and repentance for Kamini were not self-deception?

Though it was easy to think that he would keep his mind under control, it was really not so easy to do so. First and foremost, Mukunda was often cognizant that he couldn't monitor his psyche; disregarding his goals, he got irritated with discarded and disallowed contemplations and thoughts. He had even reviled himself and wanted his demise as he appeared to be unable to control himself. He was bothered because he neglected to keep his brain assuaged. In case he didn't get treatment, presumably his objective would likewise disappear like dreams, and his innumerable contemplations would orbit around his brain. Nevertheless, the extremely judicious standards and guidelines of the treatment didn't make it hard for him to remember it, nor did it allow him to lose trust in any event. He constantly remembered that his strong imagination and emotion were meaningless and not created by himself.

He tried to forget himself by different means. Realizing that he couldn't converse light-heartedly with friends or go away from time with them by playing games, he felt suffocated. He consistently kept feeling that all of them were deceiving by acting to free themselves from the incessant strain of mental debasement. Of course, he favoured the relationship between rough, guiltless, and straightforward people. For sure, even in their restricted and confined hopelessness, ailment, and anguish, all things considered, life was taken to be a pleasurable one, and happiness and distress were normal strategies for perseverance.

Apart from interacting with them, Mukunda discovered another means to keep himself distracted — reading books. He did not desire to gain knowledge, so in the beginning, he started reading shoddy novels and plays. Earlier he would have liked to read these books, but now he found it difficult. After reading some of them, his imagination turned even wilder. The ideas and feelings which he did not want to have, grew within his mind and made him weaker. After that, he borrowed a medical book from his doctor friend, and from the little bit he understood, he tried to manoeuvre his thoughts according to those lines. Unbeknownst to his knowledge, days passed in a jiffy. Once he borrowed a book on psychology from his psychologist friend, and from then, he inculcated the habit of reading this subject only. Other than this, he would also read about society, religion, fiction, politics, and so forth. He didn't read to gain knowledge but to forget everything.

But he grew knowledgeable with time. One morning while having tea, he got into a discussion on psychology with Narayan's sister Aparna. She had just appeared for her postgraduate examination on the same day and was wondering what to do next. After returning home, Mukunda realized for the first time that he didn't have any difficulty discussing the subject with Aparna. On the other hand, he was surprised that the latter was not very well versed in discovering the analytical procedure of the subconscious mind. All this while, Mukunda thought that he knew nothing about any subject.

He felt a bit strange when one day the doctor told him that he was completely cured and therefore needed no treatment. A feeling harbored akin to the sense of happiness and freedom after appearing for the last exam in college, and at the same time a little despair that everything was over.

To prove that it was a successful recovery, the doctor even told him that if he wished, he could get married once again.

After listening to him, Mukunda felt like laughing.

Kamini's elder brother worked in Patna. Her mother and siblings also lived there. Mukunda wanted to sense relief, and therefore he started harboring thoughts about how Kamini's mother and relatives had forgotten him after her death — as he didn't want to keep any contact. In addition to this, he was now an outsider to them. He had replied arbitrarily to two or three letters, but after that, he felt irritated with each letter he received. He did not open or read any letter when he saw it was from Patna.

Though he kept contact with people whom he pleased through letters, none did he receive from

Patna or write any. At the beginning of the month of *Falgun**, he received a letter from Manohar. He had taken leave and wanted to stay in Kolkata along with everyone else in the family for a month. Mukunda should therefore arrange a house for them.

The letter was full of rants. There were allegations about not keeping in touch, the earnest request to make, several major and minor arrangements necessary for their stay, and the news that everyone was worried about him. It seemed that Kamini's mother was very eager to see him for once. She would feel a bit relieved on seeing him.

Mukunda had developed a sort of relationship and understanding with the people around him after studying the wide-ranging tenets of philosophy, but that relationship was diffused by just one letter sent from his real relative. Till then, his heart that was full of indifference and dismay was quite peaceful, but it got unsettled at this once again within the vortex of real memories.

Mukunda asked himself helplessly, "Why? Why does everything have to be repeated once again?"

The next day he wrote a reply to Manohar stating that there was no need to rent a house, everyone could stay comfortably in his place. He didn't know why he mentioned the idea of staying comfortably. He probably felt that he would live comfortably in one house along with them for a month.

**Falgun: It is the eleventh month of the year according to the Bengali calendar.*

The day Manohar was supposed to reach Kolkata turned out to be very bad for him.

The compositor Kalachand was about forty years of age. He was of fair complexion, almost white. It could be assumed that once upon a time, he was very handsome. Now, of course, he had turned lean and shriveled, almost like a withered leaf. Cases of chicken pox in the city surged with the southerly winds. Kalachand's wife was afflicted with chicken pox. His children were also infected, though Mukunda was not sure about the number of children Kalachand had. A couple of days back, the latter had taken an advance of ten rupees. The amount was given to him almost out of generosity, though this tradition of giving money remained unaltered.

Kalachand did not come to work for two days. As soon as he arrived today, Mukunda summoned him.

"Kalachand, you can take leave. Come back after a month."

"Leave, babu? Will I get my salary?"

Despite having a fair complexion, Kalachand's appearance was deplorable. Had he been of a darker complexion he would not look that bad. Mukunda used to play with the bladder of a fish during his childhood, now Kalachand's face seemed to resemble the bladder of a dry fish instead of normal human skin.

"How can you get your salary? No, you won't get any. But I am not firing you. Come back after a month, and you can go on working as before."

Mukunda took a deep breath.

"Kalachand, this is the boss's order. The disease is

contagious. It is safe for you to keep away."

"Babu, my wife passed away this morning."

"Died? Oh." Mukunda fell silent.

"Babu, I came to ask for some money. I will need it for her funeral rituals. You can deduct it from my coming month's salary. And please don't give me leave, babu. I don't want that. Can we survive if we take leave?"

What could be done? How could he make him understand that if someone had such a contagious disease at home, instead of dismissing him from his job, he was being offered one month's leave without pay and that Dhandas considered it as a special favour?

"Kalachand, I cannot give you any money."

"Will the dead body rot in the house, babu?"

Mukunda closed his eyes.

"Go and take a loan from someplace else."

"Who will give me a loan, babu?" Kalachand's tone was harsh like a barking dog, though the way he said it was very normal. "My wife, two daughters, and my son have been attacked by Ma Sitala."

How were they being treated all these days? Did he leave taking loans from all possible quarters? Kalachand started laughing like a wild jackal.

"Please lend me ten rupees, babu. I will repay it to you next month by selling whatever utensils I have."

Would Mukunda give him a loan? Where will he get the money? He had to take a loan himself in the middle of the month to make the stay of Kamini's relatives a comfortable one. His salary was not enough.

"I know babu, I know," Kalachand said. The poor and innocent guy behaved as if he knew everything, and so had nothing more to add. It seemed as if he also knew that people like Mukunda even killed their wives, but when the wives of people like Kalachand die, they are not deemed important enough to get a loan of ten rupees.

Mukunda kept scratching on the blotting paper. Wife? Woman? Golden breasts, thin waist, foolish yet fearful eyes, and lips almost on the verge of crying. How cruel were they! They mesmerized men in such a way that just to keep his loss of job a secret, he had to murder them.

It was now time to go to the station. If he delayed any further, he wouldn't be able to welcome Manohar and the others who were about to arrive.

The phone rang, and Mukunda picked up the receiver to his ears. Dhandas asked, "How is the work progressing?"

Mukunda replied, "It is going on quite well, sir. One compositor has chicken pox in his house."

"Tell the durwan not to allow him into the press. Mukunda babu, you should be very strict in these matters. Let me call you Mukunda, OK? You are young like my son. I fear the ensuing sickness. Beware, don't let the guy come close to you."

"No, I won't, sir."

"Well, well. What was I saying? Oh, yes. Mukunda, today you will have lunch at my place. Please don't mind because I forgot to tell you earlier. I have a sort of aunt who lives in my house, and her daughter is going to perform a religious ritual. This is the occasion — nothing grand. Mukunda, the girl is very good. I have never seen such a good girl before."

"Yes, sir."

"I am coming. I will pick you up."

He could not go to the station. What could be done? When Dhandas himself gave him the invitation, he couldn't refuse him even if the world turned upside down. Mukunda gave a lot of instructions to Haridas, the peon, and sent him to the station. While waiting for Dhandas, he kept wondering why he was invited. Was it just for knowing about the pious deeds of a very good girl who was the daughter of his petty aunt whom Dhandas had given shelter and yet was hesitant about acknowledging? Dhandas had not only invited Mukunda to his house, but he would also come personally to pick him up in his car to keep his word.

Mukunda came to the office after lunch. But he couldn't have his meal with satisfaction in his own house because of the excitement of the arrival of Kamini's brothers and sisters. So he would be able to maintain the prestige of the invitation. But why was he being invited?

Sitting in the corner of the back seat of Dhandas's car in a huddled manner Mukunda kept on thinking about it.

After a few other words, Dhandas said, "This is the way of life, you know, this is the system. One person will earn money, and ten more will be dependent upon him. But you know, the girl is very good. She just turned fifteen and there is nothing about domestic work that she does not know. She even knows to stitch and is adept in music as well.

"Yes, sir."

"I am affectionate towards this girl. I am in search of a groom. I am an old-fashioned person, so I still believe that girls should be married off at a young age. I won't give much dowry but will ensure that the grandson-in-law becomes established and successful in life. That has to be done. It is my duty. What do you say?"

"Surely."

Mukunda was served by a slightly dark girl who was undertaking religious observance. It was not like seeing a bride, but an invitation. Was Dhandas acting as an agent of the girl or a matchmaker? But by just looking once at this young demure girl who was sweating in fear and shame, Mukunda bent his head down and tried to think how according to Dhandas he was a beggar hankering for money, a lecherous person belonging to the socially deprived class. Otherwise, how could he even think of presenting this girl in such a manner? The girl did not wear a chemise or a blouse, and the saree she wore was almost as transparent as a mosquito net. Was this Dhandas's plan? The boss was not a foolish man, for he surely knew that a man could feel excited for a brief period, but that would not act as a prelude to marrying any girl and making her a life companion.

Mukunda understood the whole affair after lunch when instead of the drawing room, he was ordered to go and rest in a very beautifully decorated room on the first floor. A hookah with lovely, scented tobacco arrived. After a few puffs, Dhandas handed over the pipe to Mukunda and told him, "Mukunda, take some rest. You can go to the press if you want to or else you can take leave for today. Let me also go and rest a little."

Soon after that, the girl, the daughter of Dhandas's aunt, arrived with a platter of betel leaves in her hand.

"Take some *paan.*"

Mukunda started to feel somewhat scared. Why was Dhandas so desperate to thrust the girl upon his shoulders so that he had even lost his basic commonsense? But did Dhandas, the slow, silent, and opportunist Dhandas, lose his mind? He never did any work before planning things. His motive of getting hold of a groom for this distantly related girl whom he had given shelter without spending much money was easily understood but Mukunda could not decipher what special plans he had chalked out to make him fall into this trap. And it wasn't clear why Dhandas simply took recourse to this crude and absurd method of exposing her to him. He was not such a naïve person. Besides, why was he so keen to adopt such an indecent method and make Mukunda dance to his tunes?

"What is your name?"

"Sudha."

"Okay, Sudha, you can go now. I don't need anything else."

"I have been asked to chat with you."

"What else have you been told?"

"He said —" Sudha hesitated for a moment and then looked straight into Mukunda's eyes and said, "if you hold my hand, then—"

"You shout."

"No, I should keep quiet."

There was no doubt that Sudha was not insane. But the way her eyes looked was nothing short of a lunatic.

It was five o'clock when Mukunda returned home. No one was inconvenienced because of his absence, all arrangements had been made and the cook and the servant had taken care of all their requirements. But there was a sort of grievance among Kamini's relatives because Mukunda did not take leave for a day and pick them up from the station. But when he told them the reason for not going to the station or even staying back at home, everyone seemed instantly appeased. His boss had invited him personally and taken him home in his car. Really, under such circumstances, how could he disobey his boss and look after other things?

His mother-in-law said, "May you live long son. This is how a man achieves success in life. If the big boss of your office is involved himself, you will rise further. You will rise much higher. If only my Kamini was alive today!"

Saying these words, she started wailing loudly for her for some time but not for very long. This was the tradition. It was the first time she was meeting her son-in-law after her daughter's death. She had started crying even before she alighted from the horse carriage and entered the house. When she went inside and did not find Mukunda there, she held back her tears. Now that Mukunda had arrived, the pending tears had to be completed.

Manohar's mother started wailing quite loudly, his wife Radharani frequently wiped her dry eyes, and his youngest brother Tamohar kept his finger to his mouth and sat down with his head bent low. About five children between the ages of two or three to thirteen or fourteen sat fearfully and stared at Mukunda with big eyes, and the latter kept staring at Kamini's sister Jamini, while she also looked at him, but it was doubtful whether she was able to see him. As her lips quivered, tears ran down her cheeks — she didn't make a noise.

Except for twins, the two sisters were completely dissimilar. Nothing — eyebrows, nose, ears, lips, chin, hair —was similar, but even then, there was some resemblance somewhere. Kamini would also shed tears silently. Jamini seemed to cry like her sister — the way she did was the same. And the physical features? They were very similar, and quite explicit. Jamini's head, neck, shoulders, chest, arms, waist, hips, knees, feet, and fingers — everything seemed like Kamini. If Jamini covered her face with both her hands, if she covered her head with a saree, Mukunda would not be able to make out whether his wife had appeared before him in flesh and blood once again.

Mukunda had not seen Jamini for a long time — almost two years. Jamini was immature then. He had never imagined that her sister would grow up with the same physical features as his wife.

Mukunda did not bat an eyelid. All the hundreds of fine dissimilarities of Jamini sank before his eyes, and she appeared like Kamini. Once, only once, he desired to embrace Kamini to his chest. He knew Kamini was not there. He knew that his wife was dead. It was he who had murdered Kamini. Even then, when Kamini appeared in front of him in flesh and blood, he wanted to embrace her at least for once.

Mukunda's head reeled, and devoid of any chairs near him, he sat down on the floor.

Then Manohar's mother stopped crying. Looking at Mukunda's face, she felt as if her son-in-law had turned insane with the grief of her second daughter. If Mukunda had lost his mind at Kamini's bereavement, if his desire for earning money and setting up a family had ended, then what would happen to Jamini?

"Let that unfortunate woman go. She had come to leave all of us in tears and has made all of us cry. Let that woman go. Mukunda, my dear son —"

He went to the press the next day. At two o'clock in the afternoon, when he called Dhandas for a very important matter, his manager informed him that the boss had not come to the office that day.

"Won't he come today?"

"No. There has been an accident in his house. Don't you know about it?"

"What is the matter? What accident?"

"That is a funny affair, sir. Shame, shame! What a time we are going through now. A granddaughter of our boss has committed suicide. I was there all this while and have returned just now."

"Who is that girl? Sudha?"

"Yes. I think her name is Sudha."

No, no, this can't be it. Mukunda felt that Sudha did not commit suicide, she had been murdered. He was startled. Murder? No, not exactly the way he had murdered Kamini. But even then it was nonetheless a murder. The difference was in the method. Instead of killing Sudha with his own hands, he had got Sudha murdered by Sudha herself. The tendency to commit suicide had acted in lieu of a weapon or poison.

A black veil was pulled back in front of Mukunda's eyes, and he saw hundreds of such murders in different ways all around him. The disease was not the reason for the death of those who died due to lack of medical treatment. Despite having doctors and shops full of medicine, if someone died instead of recovering, it was, of course, an act of killing. Those who did not have the capability of preventing disease because of the lack of nutrition in their bodies, or had lived in dirty and unventilated rooms along with many other diseases, those who did not know the easy methods of self-defense or have the opportunity or mental ability to accept it, what was their untimely death be called other than murder? In this country, this expedition of murdering people has been going on continuously and inevitably for some time. For some, it comes all of a sudden, while for some it appears very fast, and for others, it appears very slowly bit by bit. Mukunda shivered, his head reeled again.

Living among this open and enormous activity of

murder, Mukunda did not realize it all this while; seeing so many crude and untimely deaths, he could not identify them. What a strange blindness he had! Was this only his alone? Except for the definition of a few legal murders, how many people realized that innumerable murders were going on in this world continuously?

Who was responsible? Who were the people? Mukunda thought. On seeing the shriveled and half-dead people in the press, his heart became filled with an unprecedented and strong hatred toward Dhandas. He had never experienced such abhorrence in his life before. Whether it was mild or strong, he had always considered this hatred with a sense of disregard and had somehow felt uneasiness and grief. Today when his mind and heart filled with terrible abhorrence, he did not have those feelings again. Instead, he felt himself to be great and powerful and harboured an unusual sense of fixity and firmness. He had now risen far above petty personal hatred and malice. Just as Dhandas was the symbol of killing thousands of people, and Mukunda hated him because he considered him to be a representative of all those people — those who had been murdered and are being murdered — he also belonged to their group.

He summoned all the people in the press. When everyone assembled, he said, "I am leaving your press. I won't come back again." Everyone looked at him with surprise on their faces.

"Why, babu? Why suddenly?"

"Yes, I am leaving all of a sudden. I cannot be

murdered in this way. If all of you also want to live —"

No, that could not happen. His case was different. Like him, these people could not leave their jobs. They would have to go on trying to live while working in this manner, they would have to strip the power of murder and eradicate it forever.

"I am leaving my job, but I will often come and meet all of you."

Everyone started thinking about whether their manager had suddenly lost his mind. In the presence of the surprised look of the workers, Mukunda left the press slowly. He would not even tender his resignation from his job and felt no need to even inform Dhandas. He would not receive about a month's salary. But let that be. If he was in service, he would have resigned normally and left after collecting his dues, but all these days, he did not do any job. He had worked as a slave, acted as a sycophant, and had helped a murderer achieve his act.

After ages, Mukunda's felt a certain calmness today. He did not know that abhorrence could lift man to such lofty heights and could sink every sorrow, pain, turbulence, and fear. He could get rid of the continuous uncertainty of this long life. While walking on the path of life, he could feel the crowd of people in his heart. After all this while, he could feel the outsiders come inside and crowd his heart, thus making him forget the loneliness with which he had lived all these years.

He remembered Kamini. For the first time, he could undoubtedly and unhesitatingly believe that the responsibility of murdering Kamini was not his own. Those people who had helped to create a perverted and fearful ambience in his mind were responsible. He had thought how his image would fall before Kamini if she came to know he was without a job, and thus he got forced to murder her. He did not create that in his mind. But the society, education, culture, and environment — all controlled by these murderers had shaped his wrongful act.

The news shocked Kamini's mother.

"Son, you left your job?"

"Yes. From now on, I won't join any service."

Her mother thought for a while and said,

"Then son, please find a groom for Jamini."

"I will, surely."

Mukunda went on to take his bath.

Somdatta Mandal

Somdatta Mandal is Former Professor of English at Visva-Bharati, Santiniketan, India. A recipient of a Sahitya Akademi award for translation, she has translated from Bengali to English several short stories as well as different kinds of Indian travelogues of men and women during colonial times. Among them are *The Westward Traveller* by Durgabati Ghose (2010); *Wanderlust: Travels of the Tagore Family* (2014); *A Bengali Lady in England* by Krishnabhabini Das (2015), Rabindranath Tagore's *Gleanings of the Road* (2018), Chitrita Devi's *Crossing Many Seas* (2018), Hariprabha Takeda's *The Journey of a Bengali Lady to Japan and Other Essays* (2019), *Kobi & Rani: Memoirs and Correspondences of Nirmalkumari Mahalanobis and Rabindranath Tagore* (2020), and *The Last Days of Rabindranath Tagore in Memoirs* (2021). Her latest translation in 2021 is *Manottama: Narrative of a Sorrowful Wife* (1868), the first anonymous Bengali novel written by a Hindu lady.

www.ingramcontent.com/pod-product-compliance
Lightning Source LLC
La Vergne TN
LVHW090132160826
845673LV00017B/2440

* 9 7 8 9 3 9 1 4 3 1 6 4 8 *